W9-DBX-864

J 741.597 Woo
Wooderson, Philip
Guard dog

$22.60
ocm83758915
12/18/2007

DISCARDS

GUARD DOG

by Philip Wooderson
illustrated by David Burroughs
Cover illustrated by Nathan Lueth

Librarian Reviewer
Katharine Kan
Graphic novel reviewer and Library Consultant, Panama City, FL
MLS in Library and Information Studies, University of Hawaii at Manoa, HI

Reading Consultant
Elizabeth Stedem
Educator/Consultant, Colorado Springs, CO
MA in Elementary Education, University of Denver, CO

STONE ARCH BOOKS
Minneapolis San Diego

First published in the United States in 2008
by Stone Arch Books
151 Good Counsel Drive, P.O. Box 669
Mankato, Minnesota 56002
www.stonearchbooks.com

Originally published in Great Britain in 1999
by A & C Black Publishers Ltd
38 Soho Square, London, W1D 3HB

Text copyright © 1999 Philip Wooderson
Illustrations copyright © 1999 David Burroughs

All rights reserved. No part of this publication may be reproduced in whole or in part, or stored in a retrieval system, or transmitted in any form or by any means, electronic, mechanical, photocopying, recording, or otherwise, without written permission of the publisher.

Library of Congress Cataloging-in-Publication Data
Wooderson, Philip.
Guard Dog / by Philip Wooderson; illustrated by David Burroughs.
p. cm. — (Graphic Quest)
Originally published: London: A. & C. Black, 1999.
ISBN-13: 978-1-59889-829-3 (library binding)
ISBN-10: 1-59889-829-9 (library binding)
ISBN-13: 978-1-59889-885-9 (paperback)
ISBN-10: 1-59889-885-X (paperback)
1. Graphic novels. I. Burroughs, Dave, 1952– II. Title.
PN6727.W66G87 2008
741.5'973—dc22 2007006244

Summary: Ryan would rather play video games than help his dad sell artwork at the flea market. When the artwork is stolen, however, Ryan and his friend take on the case. The two boys quickly learn that a detective's work is no game.

Art Director: Heather Kindseth
Graphic Designer: Brann Garvey

1 2 3 4 5 6 12 11 10 09 08 07

Printed in the United States of America

TABLE OF CONTENTS

CHAPTER ONE 5

CHAPTER TWO 12

CHAPTER THREE 15

CHAPTER FOUR 28

CHAPTER FIVE 36

CHAPTER SIX 41

CHAPTER SEVEN 50

CHAPTER EIGHT 61

CHAPTER NINE 76

CHAPTER ONE

I didn't want to go to the flea market, but Dad saw this as his chance to stop me from playing *Guard Dog* the rest of Saturday morning.

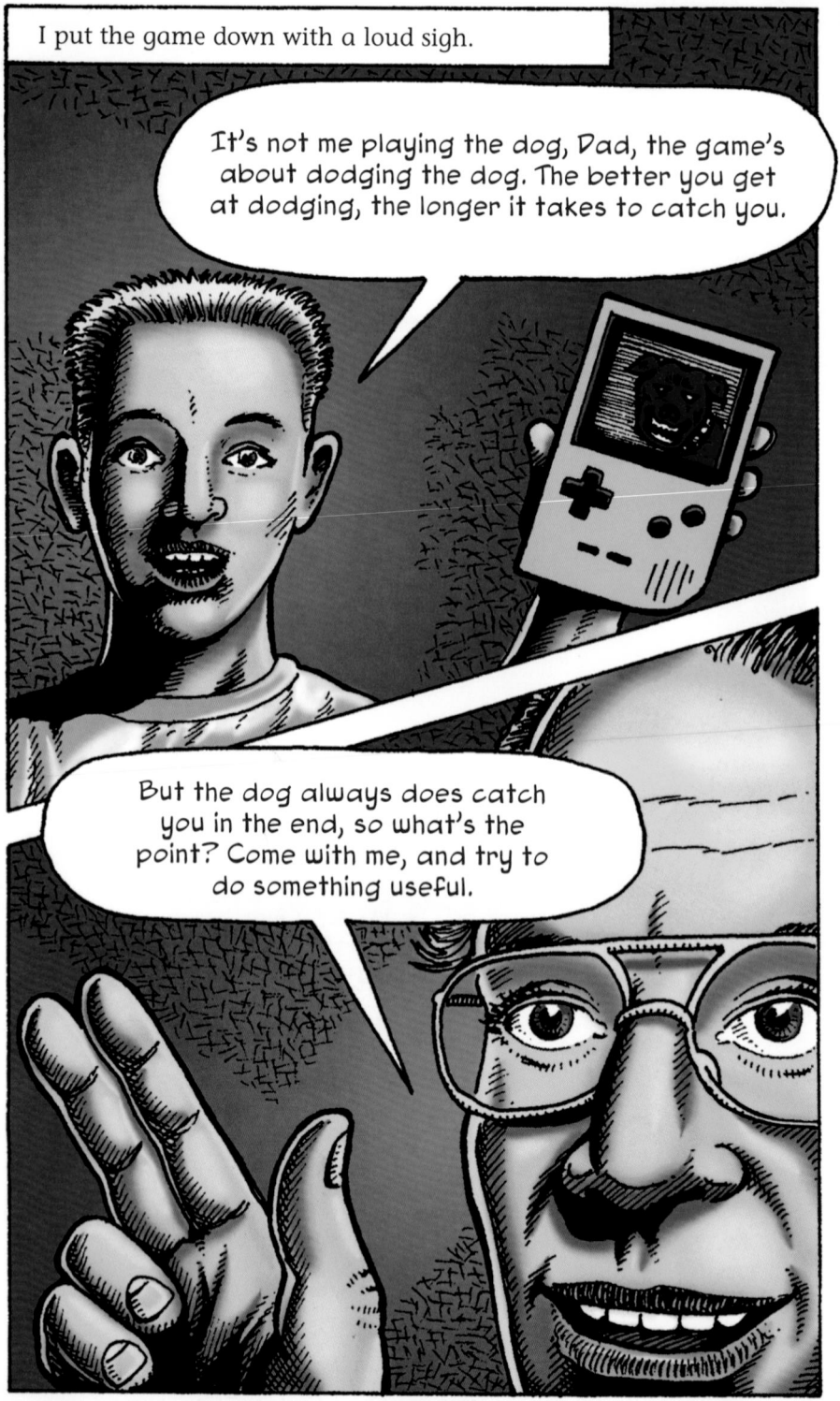
I put the game down with a loud sigh.
It's not me playing the dog, Dad, the game's about dodging the dog. The better you get at dodging, the longer it takes to catch you.
But the dog always does catch you in the end, so what's the point? Come with me, and try to do something useful.

So I went with Dad to see about renting a booth for him to sell his woodwork. Dad got the last one. He was happy until the market man told him he had to pay the rent up front.

I could see Dad was getting ready to start an argument. I gave him a jab with my elbow.

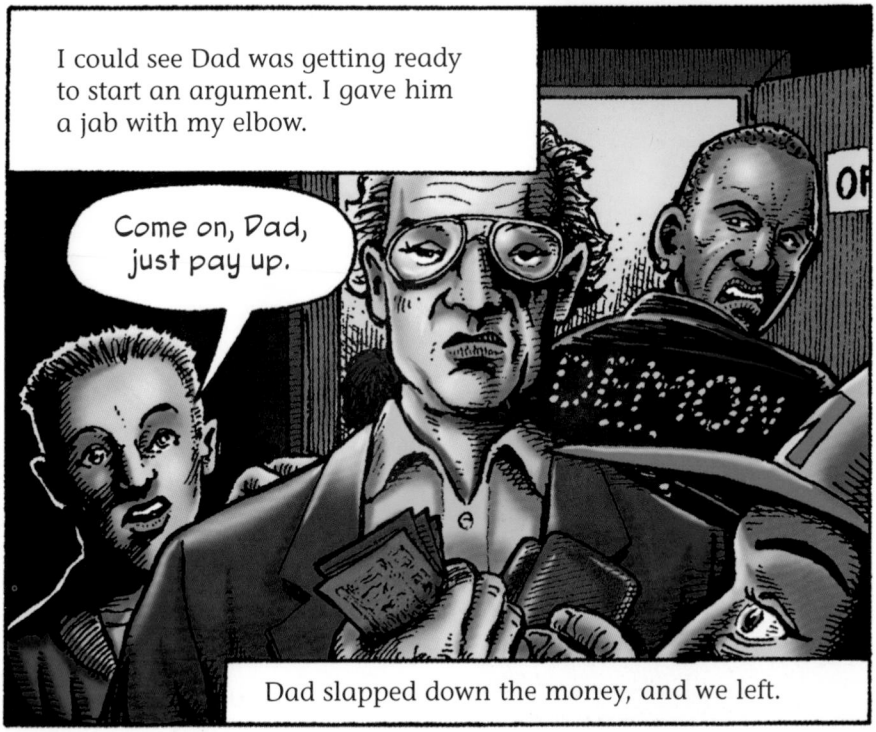

Dad slapped down the money, and we left.

Outside, a man who had been in line ahead of us caught up with Dad.

Dad had been working hard every evening for weeks turning out lamp stands, salad bowls, spoons, and doorstops.

He handed us each a card.

If your stuff's any good, I could sell it for you. That would save you the cost of renting the booth.
I thought the word "objects" had a "C" in it.
Not in the French spelling. Sounds more classy. Anyway, there's not room for two woodworking booths.
We'll see about that. *C'est un monde libre.*
Wally looked confused.
That's French for "It's a free world." Sounds more classy.
I was just trying to help. You won't last long in this game.

Dad and I drove off.
You've made an enemy now, Dad.
Life's not like Guard Dog. He can't do me any harm. Now stop worrying about Wally. You've got more important things to do.
Like what?
Like helping me load up the car.

It took me more than an hour to load the car by myself. Then I thought I'd run off to see my friend Steve. But Dad was ready and waiting.
Make sure you're back by supper. Don't want to be late tonight. You're getting an early start in the morning.
Me?
Yes, you, young man. You can help me set up the booth.

CHAPTER TWO

Dad woke me up at 5:30 the next morning.

We were out of the house before the sun came up. But our car wasn't there.

Dad quickly called the police.

My woodworking supplies have been stolen as well! I'll lose my first day of trading and the rent on the booth.

Could we have the car's license number? Then we can put out a search, sir.

The rest of the morning went by slowly. Dad thumbed through papers, and I bleeped away on my video game, trying to dodge the Guard Dog. Top score 190.

Before I could pick up the phone, it rang. Dad snatched it up.
They've found the car down by the old railroad tracks!
So, are my supplies all right? No?
But my supplies are worth more than the car and—
No, the supplies weren't insured.
Well, at least we've found your car. Could you come and collect it?

CHAPTER THREE

We found the car on a grimy street by the railroad tracks. The thief had smashed the window and hot-wired the ignition. There was already a parking ticket on the windshield.

Then we cruised around town for an hour. Dad stopped to search every alley, but we didn't find any of his woodworking supplies. Not even a single lamp stand!

As soon as we got home, Dad called the market office to tell them why we weren't there.

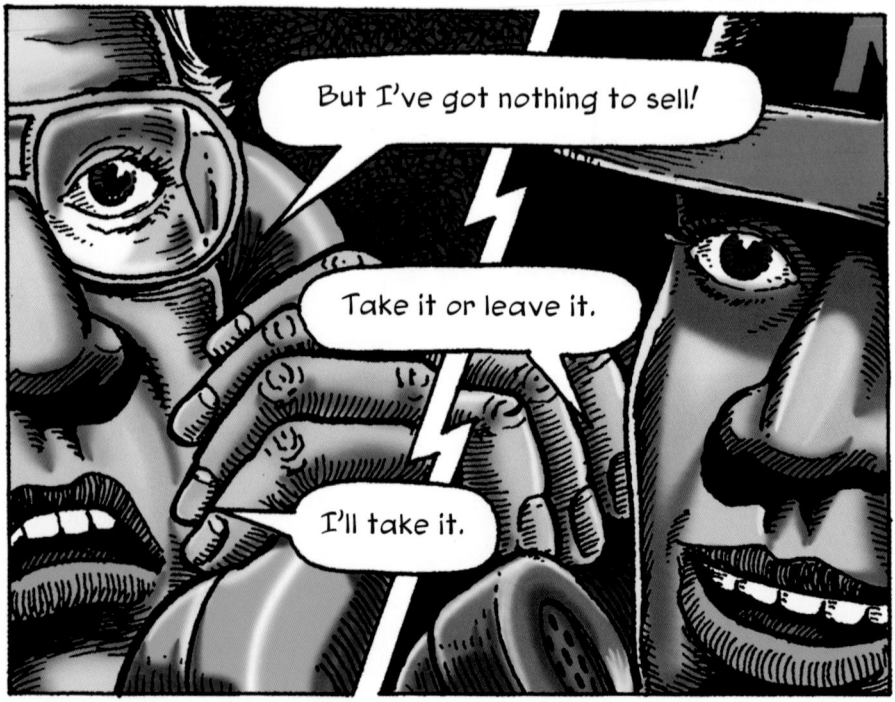

After the phone call, Dad left me in peace. He went off to the lumberyard to buy himself some more wood. When he came home, he shut himself in the work shed and got busy. Dad didn't ask me to help. After a couple of hours bleeping away at *Guard Dog* (best score 203), I was bored out of my mind.

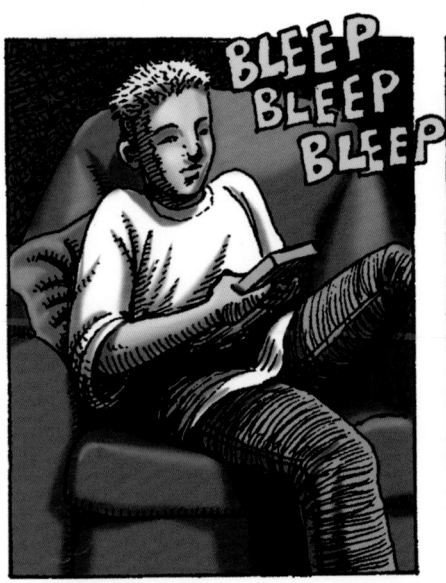

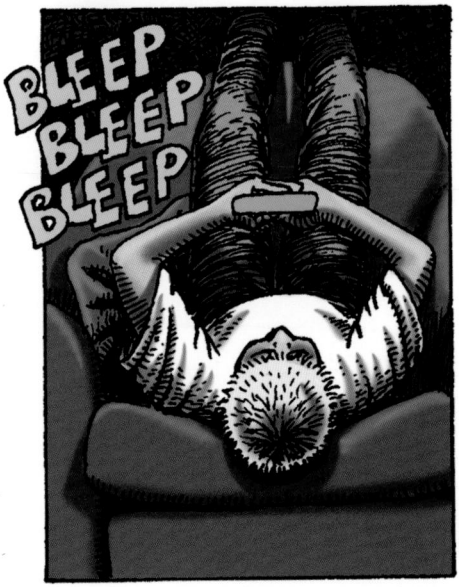

I decided to head over to Steve's house.

203, that's a pathetic score. I managed 240.
Lay off, will you, Steve? My dad's been on my case all day.
So, what did you do this time?
It's not my fault.
I told Steve what had gone wrong.

Sounds like that Wally guy might have been getting back at your dad.
What do you mean?
Come on, Ryan. What sort of ordinary car thief would go for your dad's old rust-heap?
The thief might have seen it was loaded with boxes.
Exactly. I bet he dumped them so your Dad couldn't sell them. Why else would he want loads of lamp stands?
Maybe he knew someone who'd buy them?
Why don't we go and look around the market?

In the place where our booth should have been was a big, gleaming van.
GYANT'S DISCOUNT VIDEOS
GYANT'S DISCOUNT VIDEOS
TAKE THREE U PAY 4 TWO
Your dad should sell videos, Ryan.
He couldn't make videos, Steve.

Steve picked up a video of *Death Dungeon 2*.
You're too young!
DEATH DUNGEON
DEATH DUNGEON
Yeah? Better than being too old.

We browsed around the rest of the market. Most of the booths were boring, except for one selling old comics. As we were walking toward it, Steve tugged my arm.
Look, Ryan.
Wally and Den's Wooden Objects.
WALL
WOOD
Ob-jets.
You sound just like your Dad.
WALLY & DEN
WOODEN OBJETS
Thanks.

Wally spotted us and called us over.
Your dad chickened out?

I would have told him about the car and supplies being stolen, but I noticed what Wally was wrapping.
Hey, Steve, I recognize that!

It looks like one of Dad's lamp stands!

Hey, mister, where did you find that lamp stand?
Find it? It's one of my products, and that's the last one.
What if it's stolen goods?

What?
You'd be in big trouble.
Back off, Steve.
I pulled Steve back out of range as Wally raised his fist.
The stuff's all been sold, and there's no evidence. We can't prove anything.
Whose side are you on?
Listen, Steve. My dad's not going to thank me for making false accusations.
You saw that lamp stand.
Yes, but . . .

I looked back at Wally's booth. A man in a black leather jacket was there now. Wally handed him a fat envelope. As the man walked away, I saw the back of his jacket.

We followed, keeping our distance. We watched him far ahead of us as he turned onto Main Street. For a moment I thought we lost him. When I spotted him again, he was climbing into a big black pick-up truck parked with two tires on the curb.
He looks really evil, Steve.
I bet he stole your dad's supplies.
For Wally to sell?
Who else? I think we should call the police.

CHAPTER FOUR

Back home, Steve tried to tell Mom and Dad what he thought about Wally.

A lot of people make wooden lamp stands.

Dad's are different.

Thank you, Ryan.

We saw Wally selling the last one. He got the lamp stands from Demon Den.

Dad glared at Steve blankly.

Excuse me?

I tried to remind Dad about seeing Demon Den when we had paid for the booth.

We think the "D" on the jacket must stand for Den—Wally's partner.

That doesn't mean he stole my lamp stands.
Demon and Wally are in it together. They're trying to keep you out of the market.
That's jumping to conclusions.
And why would Wally risk being caught by selling my stuff at the market?
Because he's stupid!
You boys should stop playing detective and go back to playing *Guard Dog*. Stop wasting my time.
Thanks, Dad.
There was no way I was going to tell him that we'd already called the police.

Three days later, Wally turned up at our house. He told us he'd got our address from the market office.
Have you been trying to frame me? Sending your son to snoop and telling tales to the cops?
I have no idea what you're talking about.
I peered around from behind Dad.
I thought you were selling my dad's stuff.
You only saw one lamp stand and that was half wrapped. You're a troublemaker, kid!
Ryan, I told you to stop playing detective.

That did it. As soon as Wally left, Mom was yelling at me.

When you get together with Steve, you live in a fantasy world. You don't see ordinary people. You treat them like they're all monsters in your computer game. Dad's got to get along with the other traders.

After that, I decided to stay out of everyone's way.

When I got home from school the next day, Dad was busy carrying cardboard boxes out of his shed.

But Dad wasn't worried.

I've already loaded up the car. I'm storing this stuff safely inside the house.

So what's in the car?

Empty boxes.

Clever.

Then I had second thoughts.
The thief won't know they're empty. We don't want the car to get stolen again.
That's why I'll be watching and waiting.
A moment later, he returned from inside the house with a camcorder in his hands.
I borrowed this from your uncle. If anyone snoops around the car, I'll film them and show the police.
Perfect.
Can I help, Dad? I mean, we could take turns.
I can't afford to take that risk.

Dad treated me like a child. I was feeling really down, so I went upstairs and played a quick game of *Guard Dog*. I beat my high score by 15, but what did that prove? Soon, Mom would be home, and she'd be yelling at me to finish my history project.

Suddenly, I heard someone walking up the driveway. I went and looked out of the window, expecting to see Mom or Dad. Instead, I saw a dark figure peering into our car. The studs on his jacket gleamed under the street lamp.
Demon Den!
I rushed downstairs.

CHAPTER FIVE

I should have gone and told Dad, but he was in the shed. There wasn't time to warn him. Instead I grabbed the camcorder, headed outside, and hoped that this risk was worth taking.

I didn't want Demon to see me, so I hurried through the back door and out the alleyway. By the time I got to the street, Demon was already walking away.

I trailed him for a few blocks until he stopped at a phone booth. I waited, wanting to film him, but there was no light in the booth. Fortunately, I could hear him all right, as he spit words into the phone.

Okay, so you're telling me I should have trashed the car last time? So this time I will.
It's me who's taking the risk. Why should you be worried?
No way!
He slammed the phone down and stormed out of the booth.
He walked right by without seeing me, back the way he had come from.

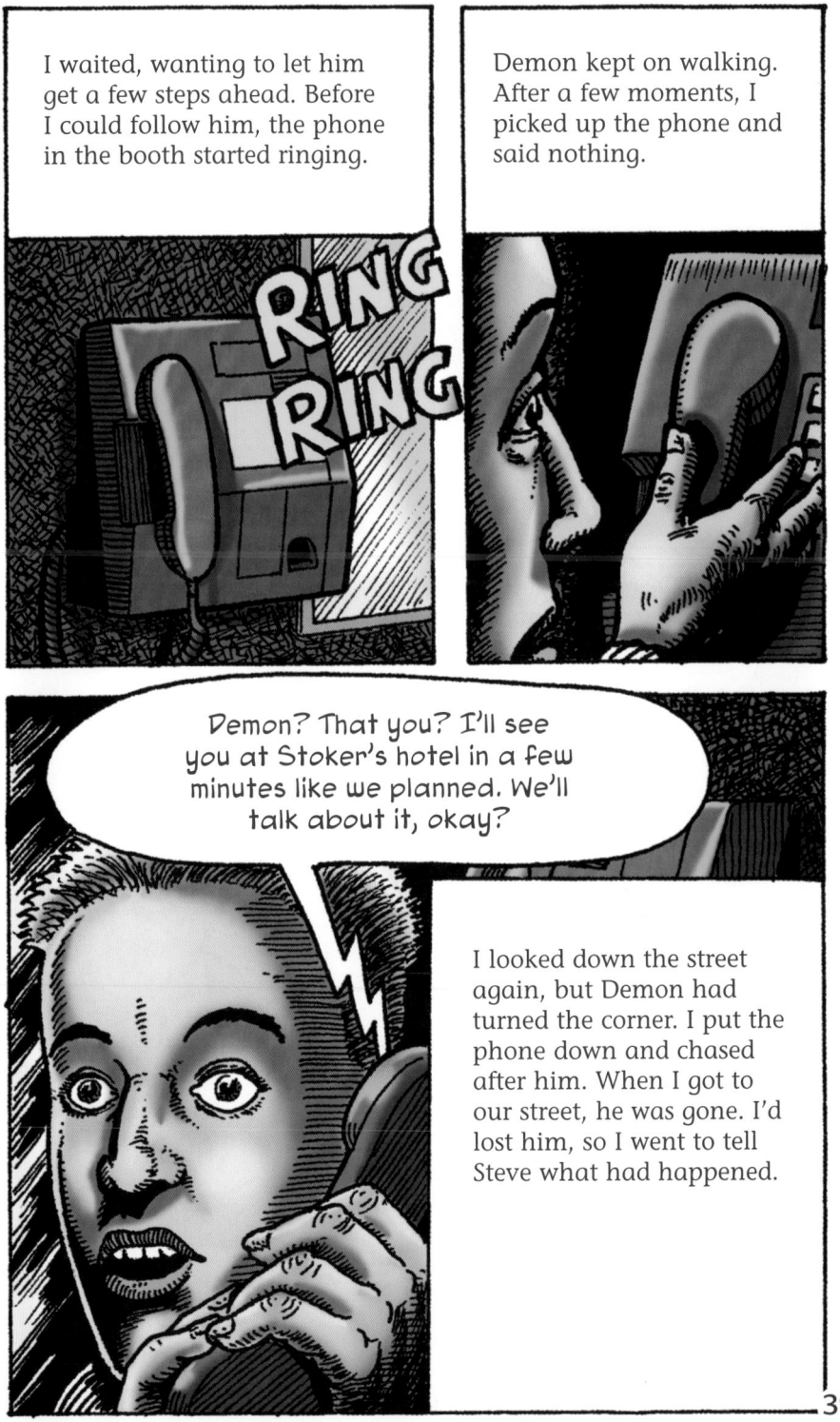
I waited, wanting to let him get a few steps ahead. Before I could follow him, the phone in the booth started ringing.
RING RING
Demon kept on walking. After a few moments, I picked up the phone and said nothing.
Demon? That you? I'll see you at Stoker's hotel in a few minutes like we planned. We'll talk about it, okay?
I looked down the street again, but Demon had turned the corner. I put the phone down and chased after him. When I got to our street, he was gone. I'd lost him, so I went to tell Steve what had happened.

It was so frustrating.
Ryan, that was clever! Now we know we were right about Den.
He wants to trash your dad's car, but Wally's afraid of getting caught.
But they're both still crooks.
Except . . .
There was something not right here.
It didn't sound like Wally's voice, Steve.
We can find out for sure.
How?
Let's stake out Stoker's! Maybe Demon will go there.

CHAPTER SIX
When we got to Stoker's, Demon's black pick-up truck was outside with two tires on the curb.
It's empty. Let's get in back.
Why?
That way we won't lose them this time.

I didn't like the idea, but as Steve climbed over the tailgate, the door swung open.

Quick!

I had no choice. I scrambled into the back with Steve.

Just keep your head down.

As we ducked out of sight, someone climbed into the pick-up's cab and slammed the door.

Suddenly, the engine roared, and the pick-up lurched forward. As the tires bumped off the curb, we got shaken and rolled all over the cold metal floor. Luckily, the journey was short.

The truck turned down a dark back street and came to a stop. Once the man jumped out, I risked a look over the side.

The pick-up had stopped outside a garage, but I still couldn't see the man's face. He unlocked the garage door. It slowly rattled open. Then the man drove the truck inside, turned off the headlights, got out, and walked off into the dark.

A door slammed at the back of the garage.

I heard someone shout: "Where's that darn dog?" Then a shrill squeaking noise as the steel door behind us started rolling down. Steve jumped out of the truck.

The door clanged onto the concrete floor.

There was no turning back. We crept along the side wall to a tall stack of cardboard boxes. Through the window of a small room, we could see two men talking—the truck driver and a small man with a moustache.

This wasn't much help. Then I remembered the camcorder in my pocket and started filming. Steve nudged me.
Do you hear that?
Dog's dangerous. You should ditch him.
I keep him for guarding this place.
But if someone breaks in, Ray . . .
He'd rip them to pieces. That's their fault.

Now Steve and I got really worried.
Suppose the dog's in here now?
I think you've done enough filming.
But I kept recording for another minute.
It isn't my style. We're not thugs. It's important we keep our hands clean.
So, how do we ditch the dog?
The thin man stood up.
A quick phone call.

Come on, Ryan! We need to hide.
Steve pulled me back behind the cardboard boxes just as the office door opened. We reached the truck and scrambled into the back before the men appeared.
They unlocked a small metal door built into the big garage door and stepped out into the street.
The door banged shut behind them, and the key turned again. A minute later, a car started up outside. We listened to them drive away.

CHAPTER SEVEN

It was still early evening. It was too soon for Mom and Dad to worry where I might have gone, and go looking for me. Steve said his parents wouldn't be home until eight. By then, Demon Den might steal our car again. Even if Dad was waiting, he wouldn't have the camcorder to record the evidence. We needed to call for help.

We've got to get to that phone, Steve.

We'll have to smash the window.

Hoping to find something heavy, I opened the nearest box, but instead of a wooden lamp stand . . .

It's full of new video tapes.

We ripped open more and more boxes. Every one was packed with identical video tapes.

Hey, Ryan, look over there.

Steve discovered a narrow space between the two stacks.

Where's that go?

The space had been left as a passage. Through the narrow opening there was a low archway, which led into a hidden room.

The room was dimly lit and filled with stacks of cardboard boxes. The far end of the room glowed with tiny red lights. There were 20 video players, all recording something. There was also a big TV and a video player on a stand.

The TV screen was blank, but the video seemed to be playing. Steve pressed the eject button.

I suddenly had an idea. Taking the tape from the camcorder, I plugged it into the player. I pressed rewind, then play, and switched on the TV.

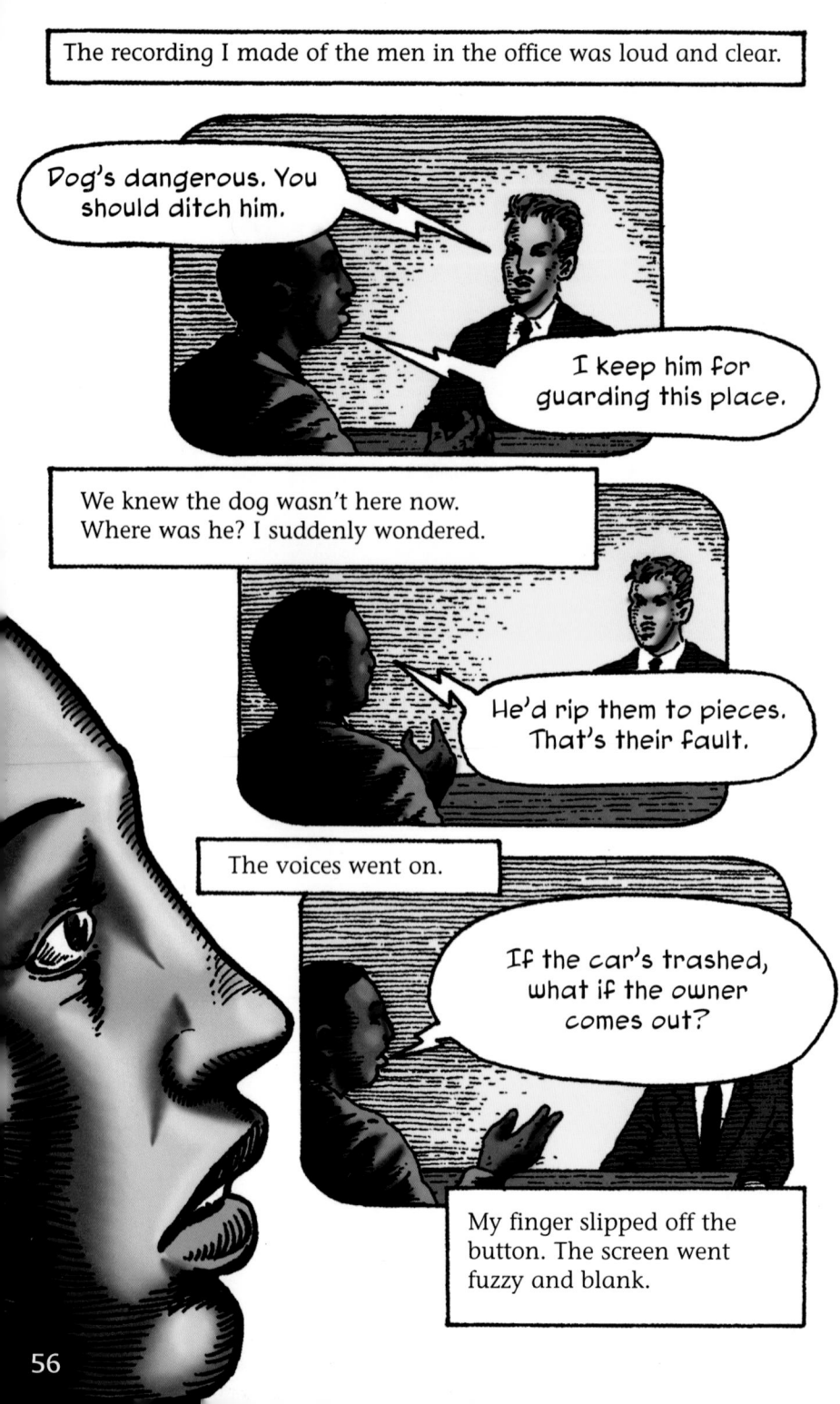
The recording I made of the men in the office was loud and clear.
Dog's dangerous. You should ditch him.
I keep him for guarding this place.
We knew the dog wasn't here now. Where was he? I suddenly wondered.
He'd rip them to pieces. That's their fault.
The voices went on.
If the car's trashed, what if the owner comes out?
My finger slipped off the button. The screen went fuzzy and blank.

What's up, Ryan?
I turned away. It was all glaringly clear.

Demon Den's got their dog.
But why is he mixed up with those two?
I mean, they're just video pirates—making illegal recordings.
I know, but you heard them talking about my dad's car getting trashed. If only we could warn him.

We can.
OFFICE
Steve found another entrance, which opened into the office from the opposite side.

I reached for the phone and dialed the number. No answer.
Call the police.

I had another idea. Demon D must have stolen Dad's car. Wally had sold Dad's lamp stands, but he might have bought them without knowing where they had come from. If so, we must have got it wrong about the "D" standing for Den. Demon D wasn't Wally's partner.

When Wally answered, I told him what we had discovered.
You mean Demon D set me up? He wants everyone to think I had your Dad's car stolen to stop him from competing with me.
Demon's out to do it again, and he's taking his dog.
Ryan, hear that?
Steve was tugging my sleeve.
Suddenly, the noise got louder, and I almost dropped the phone. It sounded like a dog.
GGG-GG-GGRRR

CHAPTER EIGHT
But instead of a dog, Demon D burst out of the darkness.
GGGG
GGRR
GRRR
Demon was growling, baring his teeth just like a—

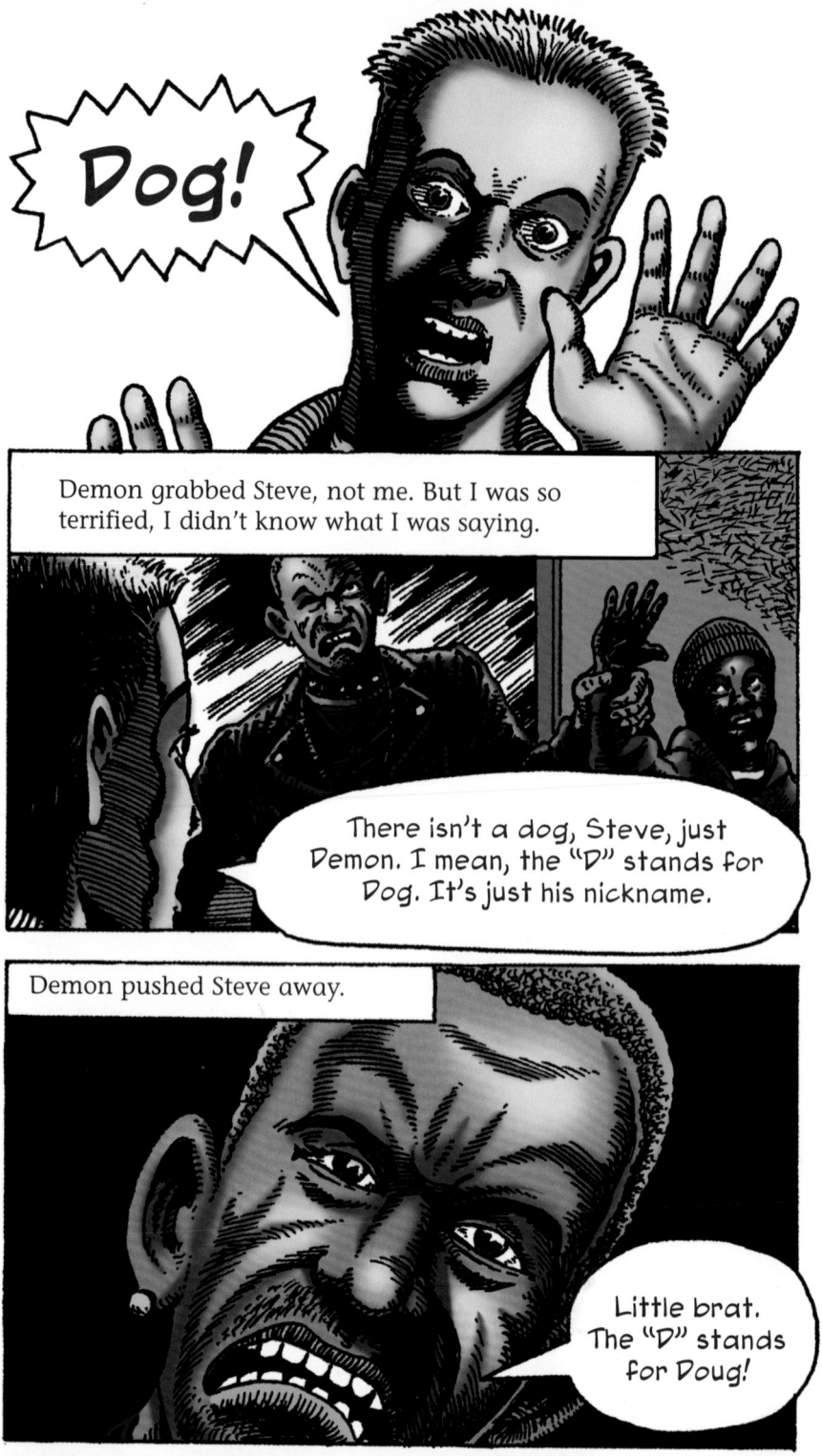
Dog!
Demon grabbed Steve, not me. But I was so terrified, I didn't know what I was saying.
There isn't a dog, Steve, just Demon. I mean, the "D" stands for Dog. It's just his nickname.
Demon pushed Steve away.
Little brat. The "D" stands for Doug!

But they called you . . .
Doug—short for Douglas.
No, your boss called you Dog!

They said, "Ditch the Dog. The Dog's dangerous."

Demon threw me back onto the ground.
They couldn't get by without me. They'd never have gotten your dad's booth without me.

And now I've caught you trespassing. Know what that means? I can do whatever I need to defend myself.

He smacked his own chin.
Ouch! You shouldn't have done that.
I stood there like a scared little rabbit.
I'll tell the cops that you started the fight!
Then Steve came to the rescue.
Run!
SLAM!

Both of us raced through the doorway, trying to dodge him like the dog in *Guard Dog*. But then Demon jumped to the right, blocking our only escape route.

Our only chance was to try to climb out of his reach.
Go over those boxes, Steve. Use the shelves as a ladder.

Demon was too quick though. He scrambled up the boxes, snatched hold of my ankle, and started to pull me down.
Run!
I tried to run, but his grip was too tight. I kept struggling but couldn't slip free. Then, suddenly . . .
YAAAHG!

He fell into the TV stand, knocking the video player and switching it on.

With Demon down, Steve and I bolted back through the passageway, across the garage, and to the exit door. Then, I remembered—the only way out would be locked.

As Demon started to get up, Steve fumbled with the exit lock. It was no use.

We ducked behind the pick-up, but there was nowhere to hide. I thought we were finished. Demon would get us for sure. Then, he'd go trash Dad's car and maybe beat up Dad too. Then I'd have ruined everything.

But weirdly, Demon ignored us. He walked straight to the door, pushed a key into the lock, and stumbled out into the street.

We followed him through the door, but he had disappeared.

Steve and I ran all the way to Main Street. In the distance, we could see blue and red lights flashing near my driveway. A police van was outside my house!

This man was shining his flashlight into my car!

I was coming to warn you and help you!
As we got closer, I could see that the man shouting was definitely not Demon.
It's Wally!
Dad, he's on our side.
You've got it all wrong, Ryan. If I hadn't lost the camcorder, I'd have the proof. And where have you been anyway?
I borrowed the camera, Dad, and I have proof that Wally isn't a crook.

To find out, we all piled into the police van and made our way back to the garage. The door was still open. As we edged around the boxes and through the hidden passageway, the room seemed dangerously quiet.

The police were more concerned with all the video recorders and what was playing on the TV screen. I had left my video in there!

Before Wally could say more, Dad apologized and asked Wally to supper. I had to wait to get the full story.

My partner, Den, was a great craftsman. He made wonderful stuff. He also took his time and wouldn't be pushed. But working six markets a week, you need a big supply. I had to buy from someone else.
That's why I bought Demon's stuff, which turned out to be your dad's lamp stands. When Den found out about my deal with Demon, he went crazy. We got into a huge argument.

So to answer your question, I don't know where Den is at. We're no longer partners.
Wally had even more surprising news.
What I need is a reliable person to supply me with classy "objets." If your dad didn't want his own booth, maybe we could work together.
You mean, you'd want to buy all my stuff?
He asked you that before, Dad, outside the market office.
Before I knew how well it sold, too. I mean it now. Be my partner.

On one condition.
Change the name to Wally and Jim's Wooden ObjeCts.
What?
The "C" is more classy. I mean, classy does have a "C" in it.
So does "clever," Dad.

Dad raised his hands with a shrug. He had to admit that our detective work had paid off.
I'm not the only clever one, Ryan. I guess all those video games must have taught you boys something after all.

ABOUT THE AUTHOR

Philip Wooderson has written more than 25 books for young people including several stories about a boy named Arf, published by Stone Arch Books.

Philip is married and has one son and one very furry cat. The family divides their time between the coastal town of Ramsgate, England, and the village of Lucignana, in the mountains of Italy.

He enjoys visiting schools and teaching writing. He also likes reading, cooking, gardening, and growing his own food.

GLOSSARY

accuse (uh-KYOOZ)—to claim that someone has done something wrong or illegal

banned (BAND)—to be stopped from doing something or going somewhere

booth (BOOTH)—a stall or stand where someone shows and sells a product

clever (KLEV-ur)—smart and carefully planned

dodging (DOJ-ing)—moving away quickly to avoid something

grimy (GRY-mee)—covered with dirt

hot-wire (HOT-wyr)—to start an automobile illegally without using a key

jumping to conclusions (JUHMP-ing TOO kuhn-KLOO-shunz)—making a decision without having all of the evidence

market (MAR-kit)—a place where many sellers gather for people to buy their goods

shrill (SHRIL)—a high-pitched sound or scream

video pirates (VID-ee-oh PYE-ritz)—people who make illegal copies of videos or DVDs

Discussion Questions

1. In the story, Ryan decides to take a risk and tries to capture Demon D on his own. Do you think this risk was a good or bad decision? What would you have done? Explain your answers.

2. In chapter four, Ryan tells his parents that he thinks Wally stole the supplies. What evidence does he have to support this guess? Based on this evidence, do you think Ryan was "jumping to conclusions?"

3. Do you think Ryan could have solved the case without his best friend, Steve? List some of the ways Steve helped.

4. Do you think playing *Guard Dog* helped Ryan solve the crime? What useful skills could he have learned from playing a video game? Have you gained any skills from computer or video games? Explain your answers.

WRITING PROMPTS

1. Ryan's friend Steve helped solve the case of the missing supplies. How have your friends helped you in the past? Pick one or two of your best friends, and write a story about how they helped you.

2. What's your favorite video game, movie, or TV show? Imagine you could jump inside your TV or video game and become the main character. Describe your adventures.

3. Demon Dog's boss nicknamed him "Demon Dog." Have you ever had a nickname? If so, write about how you got the new name and if you like it. If you don't have a nickname, make one up and describe your choice.

ALSO PUBLISHED BY STONE ARCH BOOKS

The Haunting of Julia
by Mary Hooper

Before Julia can blow out her birthday candles, the flames vanish into smoke! When she watches a replay on her dad's videotape, she sees a mysterious figure standing behind her shoulder. Julia suspects a ghost has blown out the candles and has come to haunt her.

Lost
by Chris Kreie

Every summer, Eric and his Dad head to the Boundary Waters Canoe Area in northern Minnesota. This year, Eric brought his friend Cris, and the boys want to explore the wilderness on their own. Shortly into the trip, Cris is injured, and Eric must save his friend.

Detective Files
by Steve Bowkett

Someone has stolen a priceless diamond from the city's museum! When police can't catch the crook, they call the world's most famous TV detective — Roy Kane.

Abracadabra
by Alex Gutteridge

Tom is about to come face-to-face with Charlotte, Becca's double. But there's something strange about this, because Charlotte died three hundred and fifty years ago.

STONE ARCH BOOKS,
151 Good Counsel Hill Drive, Mankato, MN 56001
1-800-421-7731
www.stonearchbooks.com

INTERNET SITES

Do you want to know more about subjects related to this book? Or are you interested in learning about other topics? Then check out FactHound, a fun, easy way to find Internet sites.

Our investigative staff has already sniffed out great sites for you!

Here's how to use FactHound:

1. Visit *www.facthound.com*
2. Select your grade level.
3. To learn more about subjects related to this book, type in the book's ISBN number: **1598898299**.
4. Click the **Fetch It** button.

FactHound will fetch the best Internet sites for you.

Harris County Public Library
Houston, Texas